Pumpkin Pumpkin

by Jeanne Titherington

Greenwillow Books
New York

WITH SPECIAL THANKS TO SAM

COLORED PENCILS WERE USED FOR THE FULL-
COLOR ART. THE TEXT TYPE IS ITC CASLON NO. 224
AND THE DISPLAY TYPE IS CASLON OPEN FACE.

PUMPKIN PUMPKIN
COPYRIGHT ©1986 BY JEANNE TITHERINGTON
ALL RIGHTS RESERVED.
MANUFACTURED IN CHINA BY
SOUTH CHINA PRINTING COMPANY LTD.
WWW.HARPERCHILDRENS.COM
FOR INFORMATION ADDRESS HARPERCOLLINS CHILDREN'S
BOOKS, A DIVISION OF HARPERCOLLINS PUBLISHERS
10 EAST 53RD STREET, NEW YORK, NY 10022
WWW.HARPERCHILDRENS.COM
FIRST EDITION
10 11 12 13 SCP 10 9

LIBRARY OF CONGRESS CATALOGING-IN-PUBLICATION DATA

TITHERINGTON, JEANNE.
PUMPKIN PUMPKIN.
"GREENWILLOW BOOKS."
SUMMARY: JAMIE PLANTS A PUMPKIN SEED AND,
AFTER WATCHING IT GROW, CARVES IT, AND SAVES
SOME SEEDS TO PLANT IN THE SPRING.
1. CHILDREN'S STORIES, AMERICAN.
[1. PUMPKIN—FICTION.
2. GARDENING—FICTION] I. TITLE.
PZ7.T53PU 1985 [E] 84-25334
ISBN 0-688-05695-4 (TRADE).
ISBN 0-688-05696-2 (LIB. BDG.)
ISBN 0-688-09930-0 (PBK.)

FOR

JAMES AND THE FISH

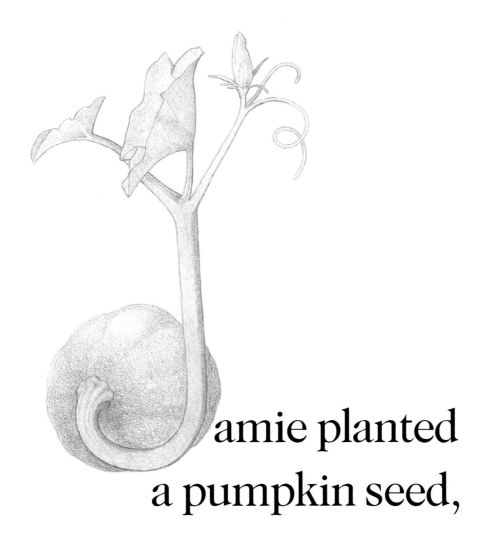

amie planted
a pumpkin seed,

and the pumpkin seed
grew a pumpkin sprout,

and the pumpkin sprout
grew a pumpkin plant,

and the pumpkin plant
grew a pumpkin flower,

and the pumpkin flower
grew a pumpkin.

And the pumpkin grew…

and grew…

and grew,

until Jamie picked it.

Then Jamie scooped out
the pumpkin pulp,
carved a pumpkin face,
and put it in the window.
But…

he saved
six pumpkin seeds
for planting in the spring.